THE TAIL OF NEKO THE JAPANESE CAT

Philip M Harris

Illustrations by Louisa Gerryts

Published by New Generation Publishing in 2019

Copyright © Philip M Harris 2019

The author asserts the moral right under the Copyright, Designs and Patents Act 1988 to be identified as the author of this work.

All Rights Reserved. No part of this publication may be reproduced, stored in a retrieval system or transmitted, in any form or by any means without the prior consent of the author, nor be otherwise circulated in any form of binding or cover other than that which it is published and without a similar condition being imposed on the subsequent purchaser.

ISBN:978-1-78955-632-2

www.newgeneration-publishing.com

New Generation Publishing

To my daughter Amy-Jo

I would like to thank Louisa for her delightful illustrations and for making my ideas of *Neko* and friends appear on the pages of this book. I would also like to thank Jacqui for her friendship and support during this project and for pushing me to complete it.

Contents

Tokyo, the Tale Begins   1

America, and the Big Apple …   5

To France we fly …   12

Next stop England …   21

Sailing the seas to Greece …   29

And then Egypt …   32

Cruising to Kenya …   38

Eastwards to China …   47

Homerun to Tokyo …   54

Tokyo, the Tale Begins

As the train slowly pulled into the station, Neko knew that his master was home and like all good cats he was waiting to greet him. The train was no ordinary one. It was the super fast Bullet Train from Tokyo which brought Mr Sato home from work every day. Neko watched the sleek blue and white locomotive glide silently between the platforms until it stopped at the red signal.

Neko was not a very big cat. In fact, he thought himself about average, as far as Japanese cats go, but he felt that his black and white coat was unusual – not many cats have one white ear and one black ear. Neko quickly washed his face with his paws, straightened his whiskers and looked out for his owner amongst the crowds of people who poured out of the carriages. It always puzzled Neko how so many people could get into such a small space. No wonder Mr Sato was always tired when he arrived home.

There he is, purred Neko, as a small, black-haired man in a dark suit and a white shirt pushed his way past his fellow commuters. Mr Sato was walking very quickly this evening and Neko had to run to keep up as they turned down a small side street towards home. Neko sniffed the air as they drew closer to their small one-storey house, trying to guess what Mrs Sato was cooking for dinner.

The tail of Neko the Japanese cat

Mr Sato noticed that the futons were still outside airing – as these Japanese beds with no legs were normally stored away in the daytime to make more space, he wondered why his wife had not put them away yet. Neko knew the answer. Mrs Sato had been very busy looking after her bonsai trees, these special dwarf trees had to have their branches carefully pruned and their roots trimmed to keep them small. Neko could never understand why they did not die from this constant cutting and trimming as he watched his mistress dig up one of these little trees and once more cut its roots.

  Later, when Neko was sleeping on his favourite futon, which Mrs Sato had kindly brought in, he was disturbed by the raised voice of a very excited Mr Sato. Neko lazily lifted his head and tilted it so he could hear what all the commotion was about. Eventually, unable to get the full gist of the conversation, he stretched twice and padded his way into the kitchen. Mr Sato was trying to explain to an extremely pleased Mrs Sato that they had been transferred to America, wherever that was.

Cats, as a rule, don't like change and Neko was no exception. He currently led a very relaxed life, wanted for nothing, his only chore to kill the odd cockroach during the summer – an arduous task, but something that was expected of a cat living in Japan. The thought of being uprooted and moved to a foreign land didn't appeal to him at all. Unfortunately for Neko, he had no say in the matter – the Satos were on the move and that included him. Later, when the family were all tucked up in bed, Neko knocked the large atlas off the bookcase to see where he was destined to go. This gesture caused fatal damage to one of Mrs Sato's beloved bonsai trees, but Neko felt that the tree wouldn't want to go to America anyway.

After a certain amount of searching, he found America on pages thirty-two and thirty-three. Even with his limited geographical knowledge, Neko realised that it was bigger than Japan and not exactly close. He wondered if they would travel there by Bullet Train, like Mr Sato did everyday. Neko, knowing that his fate was already sealed, decided to take a nap and wait to see what the morning brought – apart from the newspaper.

The next morning he realised that they were leaving soon. Strange men were coming and going, removing all the furniture, including his beloved futon. Then Neko saw it. A big box, with lots of holes in the side and a handle on the top. On each side, in big letters, was written "FRAGILE CAT". Yes, the dreaded CATBOX! With the aid of a large amount of sushi, Neko's favourite raw fish dish, he was packed into the box, destined for the airport.

Never having flown before, Neko wasn't sure what was in store for him. From the inside of his box, the plane looked very much like a short Bullet Train which had fallen off its tracks. It also had long metal arms – most odd, he thought. Neko later learnt they were called wings like a bird has. He was placed in what seemed to be a very large cupboard, with lots of other boxes and suitcases. Neko didn't need to read the large lettering on the side of his travelling companion's box to realise that he was next to a dog. How inconsiderate, Neko thought, going to all this trouble packing me into a box, making sure that I am the right way up only to put me next to a hound! To make matters worse, it whined and panted most of the way to New York. Neko decided that he would do what cats do best, so he curled up and fell sound asleep.

America, and the Big Apple ...

Much later the bumpy landing woke him. He had arrived, he was in America! His first glimpse of America was exactly the same as his last glimpse of Japan – an airport. He had to wait for a while at the airport while people who were speaking in a very funny way tried to decide what to do with him. Obviously, jet-setting cats from Japan were an oddity at John F Kennedy Airport. Luckily the Satos arrived before any damage was done and claimed him. The family headed off in a bright yellow car with a driver who would not stop talking. Later, Neko found out that it was a taxi.

Most people's first impression of America is that everything is bigger. Neko's was no different – in fact, from paw height everything looked enormous. A few days later, once he had recovered from the flight, Neko decided that this was the life. He strolled around a house which appeared to be the size of a baseball field. Exploring his new domain was actually quite exciting. It appeared to Neko that every room had another room off it and he decided that the possibilities of an enjoyable existence were endless.

Jumping up, Neko found that this cloth-covered table not only had pockets, but also coloured balls! Soon, our would-be champion had potted almost all the balls – not in the right sequence, mind you – and was about to pot the final black one, when one of his claws got stuck in the baize. He rolled head over heels and disappeared over the edge of the table. Luckily, as cats always do, he landed on all four paws – slightly dazed, however. Deciding that was enough snooker for one day, he wandered up the stairs, found a futon (with legs) and went to sleep.

Neko's new life was in every respect great. There was space to stroll, birds to chase, and bigger trees to climb – thank goodness, as the dogs were also bigger. Best of all, to deal with the cockroaches, a can of evil smelling substance killed them for him! He had retired, it seemed. Even the food was alright – except everything was served with a red sauce on it. Neko didn't feel that his beloved sushi actually required a dollop of ketchup but, taking everything into consideration, this was a minor matter.

Weeks went by and Neko enjoyed himself. Slowly, he ventured further from home, exploring the neighbourhood until one day, after a very pleasant lunch of hot dogs – a local delicacy – Neko met his first American cat. It happened on a small side street, not far from the local fish shop. The other cat was big, but then, everything in America was. His jet black coat shimmered in the sun, but what was disturbing about this local lad was what swirled behind him. The two of them stood motionless – like two gunfighters waiting for each other to draw – both staring at each other's hindquarters.

The local moggy broke the silence. "Hello, my name is Lee Roy. What happened to you?" he asked.

"What do you mean?" replied Neko, indignantly.

"Where is your tail? Who, or what, cut it off?" asked Lee Roy, turning slightly so that Neko could see his magnificent tail.

Neko was stunned. He had never seen such a thing before – except on dogs and horses. What was a cat doing with one, he wondered. The black cat sat down, curled his tail around his front paws and waited for Neko's explanation.

For a while there was an uncomfortable silence. Lee Roy leaned forward slightly, trying to see Neko's stump of a tail. This did not help matters. Eventually, Neko explained that he had recently arrived from Japan and that actually, cats from where he came from don't have tails. He went on further to explain that until he met Lee Roy, he thought that only dogs and horses had tails, something to do with flies bothering them. Lee Roy, who had hardly been out of the Bronx, obviously had no idea where Japan was. So Neko invited him home, deciding that this matter of the tails was going to have to be sorted out.

On the way, Lee Roy took him to an eating house he knew. Actually, it was around the back of a local Mexican restaurant that he frequented. "All you have to do is wait here for a while and they will serve you", he explained to our wide-eyed traveller. Lee Roy's idea of service wasn't exactly in line with Neko's. The door opened, Lee Roy ducked and the rubbish bag landed on top of Neko. "Are you alright?" Lee Roy asked as he climbed onto the bag and clawed it open. Neko shook himself.

"Yes, I'm fine," he said, following his host into the rubbish bag. The strong smell of onions, peppers and chillies made his eyes water, but he watched what Lee Roy ate and did the same. If this is what eating out in America is like, I think I'll give it a miss, he thought as he pawed his way out of the rubbish. So, having tasted a taco and some tortillas, Neko decided it was time to go home.

When they arrived home, the Satos were out. Neko knocked down the large atlas once more, almost killing Lee Roy who was waiting below for this first geography lesson. Neko paged through the large book until he found Asia, and pointed out Japan. He then went on to explain its location in relation to America.

"So that's where California is!" exclaimed Lee Roy. "My cousin went there a while ago – he is in movies – maybe you have heard of him? His name is Tom." Neko hadn't, and before he could explain any further about Japan, the Satos arrived home.

"What *is* that smell?" Mrs Sato asked.

"I think it is Neko and his new friend, and it smells like old rubbish," replied her husband.

So, quick as a flash, before Neko and Lee Roy could escape, they were picked up and taken to the bathroom. For Neko this was a weekly experience – you see, the Japanese bathe their cats regularly. Unfortunately for Lee Roy, who had never had a bath in his life before, it was quite a shock. They were dumped together into the bath and scrubbed down. Later, like two drowned rats, they emerged, were vigorously rubbed with a towel and put into the airing cupboard to dry. Lee Roy was speechless – he hated even a few drops of rain, let alone a full-blooded bath! If this was Japanese hospitality, then in future he was going to give it a miss. While they sat slowly drying, Neko decided that he was going to find out what had happened to his tail.

"Any bright ideas, Lee Roy?" he asked. His new friend had one, so as soon as they were let out of the cupboard they headed back to the atlas. After a while Lee Roy found what he was looking for – France. According to Lee Roy in France there lived very sophisticated, smart, well-groomed designer cats. Completely up-to-date with the latest fashions – perhaps a tail was a fashion accessory, Lee Roy surmised – and, if so, then the French would know where to get one.

The next day, Lee Roy introduced Neko to Danny, his older brother who lived near the airport. Danny had once told Lee Roy about a friend of his who knew how to get on flights for free. After a swift discussion, it was agreed that Neko would meet Danny and Danny's friend the following day, with the idea of getting onto a flight to Paris, the capital of France.

At home that evening, Neko wondered if he was doing the right thing. As far as he could remember, he had never had a tail. He'd never missed it, but, seeing Lee Roy sitting there all regal with his tail wrapped around his paws, was just too much. He was missing something, and he wouldn't be satisfied until he solved the mystery of the missing tail – not only for his own peace of mind, but for all the cats in Japan, who were currently living in blissful, tailless ignorance. So, early the next morning while the Satos slept, Neko headed off to meet Danny. He'd already said goodbye to Lee Roy the previous night, after a late supper at the back of an Italian restaurant.

Danny, as good as his word, had arranged for his friend to check the flight times to Paris. Apparently, one left just before lunch. Danny's friend recommended this one as it only took about five hours and it was direct, a non-stop flight to Paris. Getting on board was just a question of timing, according to the expert. So Neko waited patiently until the last of the food was wheeled on. Then, with Danny's friend's guidance, Neko snuck under the last trolley that was loaded with smoked salmon and caviar. Well, thought Neko, if this was going to be his last meal, he might as well tuck in.

The flight seems to have two classes, he noticed as he quietly moved from row to row trying to decide where to spend the flight time. According to a brochure that he read in seat 5A, the plane was called an Airbus. Clever, thought Neko, a bus that travels in the air and by far the quickest way to travel to Paris.

During takeoff, Neko had to dig his claws into the carpet to stop himself moving from 5A to 6A. The rest of the flight was rather uneventful, except for a slight commotion when the rather large lady in 5B tried to explain to a very patient and pleasant air stewardess that she had just seen a cat eating smoked salmon under the seat next to her and, what was more, it didn't have a tail! The helpful air stewardess calmed the lady down, commenting that perhaps it had something to do with the quantity of free champagne she had consumed, and perhaps another glass would see her through to Paris?

Neko decided that he should keep a low profile for the rest of the flight.

To France we fly ...

The steep descent into Charles de Gaulle airport in Paris was the only disturbance that our traveller felt after about three and a half hours of uninterrupted sleep. Much to Neko's relief, the rather large lady in 5B was still sound asleep; obviously the free champagne had worked. The landing was uneventful, and looking out of the window Neko saw the lights of Paris, the city of sophisticated, designer and chic cats. Most of all, Neko hoped for the answer to his problem. The large lady woke with a start, complaining of a rather annoying headache. The same helpful stewardess calmed her down, offering to help her off the plane. The large lady's ample fur coat was ideal cover, and soon she and Neko were being ushered through the crowds into the arrivals hall. Having no luggage and nothing to declare, Neko sauntered through the green lane into France.

What to do now was the first problem that our adventurer had to sort out. He sat for a while outside the airport building, until he noticed a local cat wearing a beret. The French cat signalled for Neko to join him next to a very big car he was sitting beside. Neko decided that he had nothing more to lose as he had already lost his tail and he walked across. As he walked towards the smoky grey cat, he wondered how he would look with a beret or a hat on, but after thinking about it he decided that he preferred people and other cats to see his unusually coloured ears.

When Neko got closer, he realised that the local cat wasn't as big as Lee Roy, but then this was Paris. He smelt of some very strong herb which Neko later found out was called garlic. Unfortunately, Neko also noticed that he had a tail.

"My name is Pierre," the grey cat said, introducing himself. "What happened to your tail?" he enquired. Neko explained again, as he had done to Lee Roy, that he didn't know why he didn't have a tail and that this was the reason why he was in Paris. Pierre decided that Neko should head for the Mecca of fashion in Paris and talk to Chantel. According to Pierre, Chantel was an expert on the latest fashions, and if a cat's tail was a fashion accessory, which frankly Pierre thought it wasn't, Chantel would know. He went on to explain that he lived with a chauffeur, which was why he was at the airport. A chauffeur, Neko found out, was a driver who picked up and dropped off important people from various places, especially airports. Neko followed Pierre into the shining black Rolls Royce and settled down in the plush interior.

Shortly afterwards, the car swept around to the front entrance of the airport to wait for their customer, who Pierre's owner had to take to the centre of Paris. The door opened and Neko couldn't believe his eyes. It was the large lady from the flight! She squeezed into the back seat, almost sitting on Pierre as she completed this awkward manoeuvre. Pierre and Neko moved to the other side of the back seat and settled down once more. The first thing the large lady did was use the car phone. It seemed that she was arranging dinner for this evening, while complaining about the flight over from New York, saying something about a cat in the seat next to her. Finally she finished her call and started to read a fashion magazine. Neko tried to see if there were any pictures of cat's tails as she paged through the glossy publication. Unfortunately there weren't any, and Neko wondered if he really was going to find the answer to his problem in Paris.

Having dropped off the large lady, Pierre and Neko waited until the limousine stopped to be cleaned prior to its next employment. Once the car arrived at the car wash, they got out and headed for the area of town where Chantel could usually be found. On the way, Pierre offered lunch and Neko was relieved as he was actually quite hungry.

They stopped outside a small café. Pierre explained that Maurice lived here and that it was one of the best places in Paris for bouillabaisse, which turned out to be a type of fish stew. It appeared to Neko that all the streets in Paris were lined with small cafés. People passed time sitting outside these places drinking wine and talking. Neko thought that this would be a very good idea for the streets of Tokyo, if it had the space.

Maurice arrived carrying a long French loaf of bread, which he called a baguette. Soon they were like everyone else along the street, sitting, talking, drinking and munching on lumps of bread, while they watched the world go by. Maurice was great company; every time he talked he waved his paws in the air and explained that garlic was very popular and quite healthy. Yes, it did smell but if you ate some yourself, you couldn't smell it on others. The three of them sat under a table in the sunshine, while Pierre explained to Maurice what Neko was doing in France. Maurice actually said that, apart from the fact that Neko was obviously a cat, from a distance he could be mistaken for one of those horrible small dogs that the English royal family had. He pointed out that sometimes the café had to put up with those dreadful people from across the other side of the Channel, the English. Some of them even had these small dogs as pets!

After lunch, Maurice took them around the back of the café, and once inside he showed them where England was, using an old map on the wall. No wonder they have small dogs, thought Neko. It's a small place. Pierre commented that should Neko wish to visit England, there was a tunnel that went under the sea which was really the only direct way into that boggy island. The alternative was to live in a small cage for six months called quarantine before being allowed to enter England. Neko didn't like the sound of that at all so he made a note that should he have to go to England, he would use the tunnel that the French cat had mentioned. Pierre went on to explain that the English were always worried about the spread of a disease called rabies which caused animals to go mad and also affected humans. Actually, Maurice and Pierre thought that the English already had rabies as they acted so strangely whenever they came over to France. Having relaxed with Maurice for a while, Pierre decided it was time to try and find Chantel. They left Maurice asleep in the sun and made their way to the fashion district.

It took them a few hours to find Chantel. As always, she was busy, advising somebody or catching up on the latest fashion gossip. The streets in the fashion district were totally different from where Maurice lived. The streets were lined with very expensive shops, all with bright display windows, each shop trying to persuade shoppers to come in. Chantel was watching a fashion show in one of the famous shops. They were ushered into a small room with lovely old chairs. Pierre jumped up onto a large soft one, while Neko decided that the floor was better for him.

The door opened and Chantel came in. She was beautiful. Pure white, with a very small pink ribbon around her elegant neck. She purred a greeting to Pierre and slowly sauntered up to Neko. Pierre had obviously mentioned the reason for the visit because she slowly walked around Neko and stopped to study the source of this strange problem. Neko waited as she slowly and elegantly strolled across to a table near where Pierre was sitting. On the table was a very large collection of fashion magazines. With a practised paw, she slowly paged through a few. "Unfortunately, Neko," she began, "cat tails are not a fashion accessory. The closest I can suggest is a fur wrap made from a fox's tail." When Neko saw the picture, he was sure that it was not what he was looking for. Firstly, it was the wrong colour and secondly, it was far too bushy for Neko. Chantel agreed that a fox tail didn't suit Neko. So, the three of them sat there until Pierre mentioned the dogs in England.

"Have you ever seen one, Chantel?" Neko asked.

"Yes, I have. Sometimes people come into the shops with them. Maurice is right, they don't have tails. Perhaps they could help Neko. As the English have dogs with no tails, perhaps they have cats as well. If not, then maybe they could point Neko in the right direction to find a solution to his problem," Chantel said.

Pierre explained to Chantel about the tunnel they now knew about. She promised to check with her brother who, unlike her, lived with a man on the coast of France. Neko and Pierre left the plush surrounds of Chantel's shop, agreeing to meet her later – once she had contacted her brother.

Night approached and the lights of Paris started to twinkle. As our pair of friends walked through the busy streets, they rounded a corner and Neko stopped. "Look! It's Tokyo Tower!" he exclaimed, pointing at a brilliantly lit metal structure. Pierre laughed. "That's the Eiffel Tower, one of our most famous landmarks."

"Well, that may be so," said Neko, "but we have one exactly like it in Tokyo." Thinking about it made Neko homesick. Oh, to be back in Tokyo, curled up on a futon after a delicious bowl of sushi! They sat for a while looking at the famous sight, both feeling proud of their respective towers, even though they were on different sides of the world.

Pierre decided that his new companion needed cheering up, so they went to see Jean Paul who Pierre was sure could do the job. Jean Paul lived with a very funny man who pretended to act like various things. The strangest thing was that he never made any noise. Jean Paul said it was called miming. When they arrived, Jean Paul was watching his master performing to a small group of people. He invited them in and soon Neko was laughing. The man was very funny, especially when he pretended to be a dog. He looked so stupid – just like a dog – sniffing around, barking (but with no noise) rolling over, doing the usual things that dogs do. Later, the three of them – Jean Paul, Pierre and Neko, went to see Maurice and have supper.

Maurice had laid on a special meal for his foreign guest – frog's legs. Neko had caught a few in his time, just for fun, but he had never thought of eating them. Well, apparently in France they are a delicacy. It did puzzle him that they only eat the legs, which didn't have much meat on. They tasted just like chicken, Neko thought after eating a few. Having finished his meal, Neko bid Maurice farewell and headed off with Pierre. They walked through the streets, which were still very busy, to wait for Chantel to contact them. Neko slept well that night – even though Paris hadn't provided the answer, another possible area which might have the solution to his problem was in hand. England.

When Pierre woke Neko, Chantel had already called. She had arranged for her brother to meet Neko at Calais, which was on the French side of the tunnel. Pierre checked his owner's schedule and luckily he was going to the railway station in the morning to collect a package for a client. They arrived at the garage just in time to get a lift to the station. Pierre explained that it would take quite a long time to drive to the station as the traffic in Paris was very heavy. Neko decided not to tell him that the traffic in Paris was nothing like the problems in Tokyo. He looked out of the window instead and watched the small Tokyo Tower go by. Pierre wished he could go on with Neko to the coast, but unfortunately his owner had earlier complained about rats in the roof, so Pierre really should get back to his duties after putting Neko on the right train. Actually, it was ideal that they were going to the station to collect a package, because the collection point was right next to the line that led to the coast.

There was no time for goodbyes as the train was about to leave. Neko jumped up into the mail van as it was pulling out of the station. He settled down amongst the mailbags wondering if he would ever see his newfound friends again. The post that Neko was sitting on was bound for London. Would these letters arrive before him, or would they also have to wait six months before being allowed into England? The trip to the coast took a few hours. Neko slept well – perhaps it had something to do with the gentle rocking of the train as the coach went over the gaps in the track. It made a click-ity-click noise, which was very soothing. Pierre had told him that as Calais was the last station on the line, there was no problem of oversleeping, but Neko woke about half an hour before the train pulled into the port. As the train approached the port, Neko saw the sea for the first time. Was he actually going to travel UNDER that mass of water? The thought did frighten him, but it seemed to be the only way for him to get into England.

Next stop England …

Chantel's brother was waiting. He also wore a beret like Pierre but his was red and his green eyes were very friendly. His white fur was covered in dust and pieces of straw from where he had been sleeping on a bale of hay. He looked so down to earth as he explained to Neko that the tunnel was a few miles away. Neko noticed he smelt not of garlic as Pierre had done, but rather of onions. It turned out that he lived with an onion seller. They climbed into the basket on the front of the onion seller's bike and set off for the tunnel. Chantel's brother wasn't sure when the tunnel had been completed, but felt it would be safe enough for Neko's purpose.

Eventually, after many stops to sell their wares, they arrived in Calles. Neko headed off towards the town centre looking for the tunnel entrance which he found behind a small station. Between the station and the sea Neko saw a large hole in the shoreline; the train track disappeared down this hole. I am glad I don't have to walk, he thought to himself, it looks like a long way to the other side. As it turned out, he didn't. A train pulled into the station and an assortment of cars and trucks drove onto the train via a clever series of ramps. Neko slipped into the cab of a small wagon and soon he was on his way to England.

Neko felt like a mole as he emerged at the other end of the tunnel. His first view of England was rain, but he had been warned about that. He left the warmth of the van's cab and made his way through the rain to a small shed. Through the window he saw four people sitting around a fire drinking a light brown liquid. Then Neko saw what he was looking for – another possible friend. On a tatty rug in front of the fire was a cat. It was sound asleep and looked very content. It was a mixture of colours which Neko later found out was called 'tabby'.

Neko waited for about an hour; then the men began to moan, picked up their hats and went outside. The cat didn't move. Neko quickly slipped in through the open door. The shed was dry and warm – no wonder the cat didn't move, thought Neko. He sat for a few minutes, then, clearing his throat, tried to introduce himself. The local cat twitched one ear, slowly turning her head. She (her name was Tabatha) lived mostly in the shed, due to the constant rain. "You look frozen," she said, as she poured some hot milk for Neko. They talked for a while before Neko realised that she didn't stare at his stump like the others had; she didn't even ask him what had happened. She just talked about the weather and other simple things. Finally, Neko got up and started to explain his problem. At the end he slowly turned around and showed Tabatha his stump.

She didn't really seem at all interested, until he mentioned the dogs that the royal family had who were in the same unfortunate position as him, tailless. Suddenly, she was a changed cat – she sat upright, her head held high, and took him around the back of the shed into a small room where she kept a few books. Tabatha was actually a royalist; she had books and pictures and her hero was a cat who had been to see the Queen who had frightened a mouse from under her chair. She was very excited about the possible prospect of going to see the Queen herself, and promised to help Neko in any way she could.

They went back into the shed. "You must be thirsty," Tabatha said. "How about some tea?" Neko couldn't believe his luck! He hadn't had tea since he left Japan! He licked his lips. Yes! Green tea, that very refreshing drink we have all the time in Japan! Unfortunately, Tabatha's idea of tea was very different. Firstly, she poured some milk into a small cup and saucer and then she added some of the hot dark brown liquid that the men had been drinking before. Finally, she added some white grains of something that looked like salt. "There is nothing like a hot cup of tea," she said as she passed Neko the cup. It smelt very sweet and tasted even sweeter. Neko wondered what green tea would taste like with milk and he concluded that the two variations of tea should not be mixed.

By the time Neko had finished his tea, Tabatha was already planning their journey to London. The simplest way was by train. They would get to London within a few hours. So that evening they caught the train to London. Tabatha had arranged to spend the night with a friend of hers called Marmaduke, who lived in Mayfair which was very close to Buckingham Palace, the Queen's London residence. "How will we know if she is in?" asked Neko. "That's easy," explained Tabatha. "According to Marmaduke, when she is at home her flag flies above the palace. Marmaduke checked this evening and the flag is flying, so she is in and consequently those little twits called corgis are as well, the dogs without tails that you wish to see."

London was full of very interesting sights: red buses, black cabs, lots of old buildings and a very large shiny steel wheel that was next to the river. The wheel (called the "London Eye") had capsules around the rim that visitors rode in and viewed the city from. Neko preferred the viewing towers that Tokyo and Paris had; at least they stood still.

Before meeting their host for the night, Tabatha explained why he was called Marmaduke; his coat was orange (similar to marmalade) and he was owned by a duke, so the name Marmaduke suited him down to the ground. He was waiting for them on the steps outside his master's very plush house. He looked very similar to the much larger stone cats they had seen earlier in Trafalgar Square that guarded a small tower with a man on top. Tabatha explained that they were called lions and they lived in Africa, where they ruled as kings of the jungle. Neko hoped he wasn't going to have to visit the King of cats to solve his problem, especially as he didn't know where Africa was. Tabatha was right, his fur did look like the colour of marmalade and his long tail that curled at the top looked like a stick of orange candy. Marmaduke ushered them inside and walked through the many rooms as if he owned the place, until he came to a small room which was like a museum with lots of old suits of armour and coats of arms on the walls. It was here that Neko experienced his second encounter with English tea. This time it was served on a silver tray, from a silver teapot. When eventually the subject of Neko's visit to London came up, Marmaduke was as well-mannered as Tabatha had been and he didn't stare at Neko's stump. He listened quietly and then went over to the bookcase. With much more skill than Neko usually used, he pulled down a few books.

Under 'C', Marmaduke found 'corgis' – described as small Welsh dogs favoured by the British royal family. They were also called 'man's best friend'.

"Why are they called that?" asked Neko.

"Well, I think it's because they are stupid; they follow people around all day long and do stupid things like carry the newspaper and slippers in their mouths," Marmaduke replied.

The most interesting part for Neko was a picture of these curious animals. Sure enough, they had no tails, just small stumps – just like Neko. After consulting various other books and some more tea, it was agreed that Marmaduke would take them down to the Palace tomorrow. Marmaduke had a friend called Busby. He lived in a guard house next to one of the gates and was sure to be able to get Neko a reception with one of these corgis. Marmaduke felt, having already met one of these dogs before, they were unlikely to be able to help Neko. His personal opinion was that the answer lay with the great old cats of Greece. He had read a while ago that there lived in Athens two very scholarly cats called Playcat and Arcatmedes. The three of them – Neko, Marmaduke and Tabatha – studied the large atlas. It appeared that Athens was a long way from London. Marmaduke concluded that, as they were both ports, the easiest means of transportation was by ship. Neko hoped that 'man's best friend' was going to be his friend as well and solve the problem of his missing tail as he had no interest in sailing.

After a breakfast of toast and marmalade and more tea, the party set off for the palace. They found Busby asleep inside one of the guard houses. He confirmed that 'those dreadful yappy things', as he called corgis, were inside. So, with Busby at the head, the column marched straight up the red carpet into the palace. Within a few minutes they found the corgis. Neko was relieved to see that they had no tails. Unfortunately, they didn't know what had happened to their tails – in fact, they didn't know much at all.

The only member of the group who was pleased was Tabatha. She went into the throne room full of gold and sat under the Queen's chair. There wasn't a mouse to frighten, but she had sat on the same spot as her hero had years before. They left Tabatha purring under the throne, dreaming of her ideal tom. Busby led them out through the gates into the busy streets outside the palace. Neko sat down; he was really fed up. Marmaduke thanked Busby for his help and then set off with Neko back to his house. They had a dinner of salmon and milk and settled down for the night. Marmaduke rightfully felt that Neko was tired and no plans or decisions should be made until after he'd had a good night's sleep.

Neko did sleep well. He didn't wake until he smelt fresh toast. He opened his eyes and noticed that Marmaduke was studying a newspaper called Lloyds List. Neko later found out that it was a daily shipping newspaper that listed the schedules of vessels all over the world. Marmaduke's paw was on the page covering Greece, which had a very busy port called Piraeus. He was checking to see when the next vessel was due to leave Tilbury Dock, in London, for Piraeus. Neko realised that the decision had already been made. He had started this trip, which was turning into a pilgrimage, and he couldn't stop until he had solved the mystery of the missing tail. He ate his toast and drank his tea while his host planned his journey to Greece for him. According to the newspaper, a ship called *Tokyo Maru* was sailing tomorrow morning directly to Piraeus. What's more, Neko pointed out, the ship in question was a Japanese one! Could there be some of his beloved sushi on board? He hoped so.

With a day to kill, Marmaduke showed Neko the sights of London. They walked along the River Thames which flows through the city. Neko saw the Tower of London and, next to it, Tower Bridge that opened in the middle when large ships had to pass through. In the evening, Marmaduke took Neko to see a show that Neko thought wonderful – it was by a man called TS Eliot and was called 'Cats'. There was a lot of singing and dancing but, alas, all the cats DID have tails.

Bright and early the next day, Neko set off for the docks. Marmaduke had arranged for a friend to escort him down to the wharf where hopefully they would be able to sneak Neko on board the *Tokyo Maru*. When they arrived, to Neko's relief, she was still there. He was even more pleased to see the Japanese flag flying from the stern. Boarding the ship was slightly dangerous as Neko had to climb up one of the mooring ropes that held the ship in position against the dock. Luckily, with the aid of his strong claws, Neko was able to climb up and onto the deck. He quickly found a safe place to hide until after they were at sea. Then he would try to find somewhere more comfortable for the duration of the voyage from England to Greece which would take about a week.

Sailing the seas to Greece ...

Neko waited almost a day before he ventured out from his hiding place. By then the ship was well on its way. He was hungry, so the first place he set out to find was the galley, which is what kitchens are called on ships. Neko did what most cats do – he followed his nose. He soon found the room he was seeking. Looking in, Neko couldn't believe his eyes! On the table was a pile of fresh sushi! He licked his lips and was about to jump up on the table when he was hit from behind. Suddenly, he found himself rolling over and over down a corridor, with something on top of him. Neko wasn't used to fighting, so he was easily pinned down to the deck by none other than another cat.

"What are you doing on my ship?" demanded the other cat. Neko struggled to get up, trying to explain why he was on board. Then Neko noticed something very odd. The cat that had attacked him didn't have a tail either.

"Are you from Japan?" he asked.

"Of course," replied the other cat, "this is a Japanese ship."

"So am I," said Neko. He then explained why he had stowed away on the ship. The other cat apologised for attacking him, but explained that he was only trying to protect his sushi.

"Was Neko hurt?" asked Kenji.

Neko replied that he was not and the ship's cat was glad.

"Sometimes I forget how strong I am. You see, I learnt judo when I was a kitten as a form of self defence against bigger cats and dogs," explained Kenji.

Neko knew all about judo, the Japanese art of unarmed combat, and wished he had learnt it when he was young.

In light of the fact that Neko was also from Japan, Kenji was very willing to share his sushi. Kenji, as Neko later found out, was from Kobe, a large port in Japan south of Tokyo. He had been with the *Tokyo Maru* for just over a year; he had travelled all over the world and knew Piraeus quite well. After some delicious sushi, Neko explained that he was trying to find out why he and Kenji had no tails. Kenji did admit that it bothered him sometimes, but as he stayed on board the ship most of the time, no other cats saw that he had no tail so he really didn't mind being without a tail.

Neko and Kenji became good friends during the steaming time to Greece, and when they eventually arrived, Kenji introduced his newfound friend to Dimitri, a local lad who obviously knew his way around Athens. Neko explained that he wished to meet the two scholarly cats, Playcat and Arcatmedes. Dimitri confirmed that they could usually be found in the evening up at the Acropolis, discussing various theories they had, about many subjects, but that would only be after dinner, and dinner was always late in Greece. So, Neko followed Dimitri through some small back streets to a small café where they could eat and relax until it was late enough to go and find the local scholars. Neko soon realised that there was little to hurry about in Athens. On the way to the café, Dimitri stopped on numerous occasions to greet and chat with relatives and friends – it seemed to Neko that most cats he met were related to his guide. A few of them had pieces missing, like the odd ear, or looked very tatty, but unfortunately for Neko they all had one thing in common with every other cat he had met, excepting Kenji – they all had tails.

After a long meal of bread, cheese and olives, they eventually wound their way up to the Acropolis. It stood in the middle of Athens looking down on the city, and even though it was, for all intents and purposes, a ruin, it looked majestic enough for Neko to stop in his tracks and admire it in the moonlight. Sure enough, our two scholars were already in deep discussion on a subject that Neko didn't understand. There was a group of cats sitting around listening and learning from the wise pair. Upon Neko's arrival, he was ushered into the centre of the gathering – Athens was really just like a small village and Neko's arrival and problem were soon common knowledge. Playcat spoke first, very slowly and clearly. It seemed that Neko's problem was something that neither he nor Arcatmedes could do anything about. Arcatmedes explained that in his opinion, Neko should go back in history to the most famous cat in the world, which had lived in Egypt. Actually, she wasn't a real cat at all, but one made of stone. The Sphinx was her name and she could be found across the Mediterranean Sea near Cairo, the capital of Egypt.

"That," concluded Playcat, "is the only help we can really give."

Neko sat for a while, listening to the group discussing his problem, but since no one else came up with any other bright ideas, off to Egypt it was.

And then Egypt …

Luckily, the *Tokyo Maru* was still in port. So, with Dimitri's and Kenji's help, Neko found himself back in small Japan. Kenji consulted the sailing schedule that was in the captain's cabin. The ship was on its way to Japan, but luckily it would have to pass through the Suez Canal, which belonged to Egypt. A few days later Neko, refreshed with sushi, disembarked in Port Said, at the beginning of the canal.

The day before, Kenji and Neko had searched the cargo hold of the ship, looking for some cargo that was destined for Cairo. They soon found a tractor, and a few hours before the ship docked in Egypt, Neko climbed into the cab of the tractor and settled down for the trip to Cairo. He was sad to leave Kenji and this small, floating Japan but he was going to find out what had happened to his tail and that was that. Neko asked Kenji if he would like to join him, but Kenji declined saying that shore life wasn't for him. He added that if Neko solved the puzzle of the missing tails to please tell him the answer. Neko promised that he would.

The journey from Port Said to Cairo was very simple. Neko stayed on the tractor, which wasn't difficult as he was in the driver's cabin. Eventually, Neko arrived in a huge market place and he soon spotted what he was looking for – a local cat. The local lad was sitting on a cushion watching the world go by. Neko was most intrigued by his hat which reminded him of a flower pot, except that it had a tassel hanging down the side from the middle – later, Neko found out it was called a 'fez'. Ahmed, the local cat, knew where the Sphinx could be found, which wasn't surprising as it hadn't been moved for thousands of years.

They made their way south from Cairo, the longest river in the world

– the Nile – to Giza. Neko noticed some very large stone triangles, which Ahmed pointed out and told Neko they were called pyramids and they were the tombs of the pharaohs – the ancient Kings of Egypt – built thousands of years ago. Neko knew there were similar old tombs in Nara, the old capital of Japan, but not as old as these were. Neko realised that he was in a very old country indeed and surely the answer to his problem was here, somewhere.

The Sphinx was magnificent though weathered by age and the wind and rain. She lay amongst the pyramids, watching the river of tourists flow slowly by, paying their respects to a civilisation long gone. Neko stood admiring her and pondering how he was going to ask such an enormous animal such a small question. Then Neko noticed that this famous cat had something missing too – her nose. Neko's hopes rose; perhaps this missing nose could be connected to his missing tail! When Neko asked Ahmed, he laughed. "I think not, Neko. You see, the Sphinx's nose was shot off by the French army of Napoleon Bonaparte, who used the Sphinx as target practice." Still laughing, Ahmed adjusted his fez and padded off to find the keeper of the Sphinx. She was called Cleocatra and with a bit of luck, she would be able to help.

She was found sitting in exactly the same position as the Sphinx, in the shade of a palm tree. When Neko walked in, she noticed immediately that something was amiss and asked him to turn around. She studied Neko for a while, and then disappeared in a puff of smoke. Neko and Ahmed, minus his fez, hid in a large vase and only came out after another puff of smoke and Cleocatra's assurance that it was safe to do so. Unfortunately, even with all her magic, she had to admit that the Sphinx was unable to help. The only assurance the Sphinx would give was that there was an answer to Neko's question; he would find the answer in the end, as long as he was willing to persevere.

Neko sat with Ahmed under a palm tree, eating the dates that had fallen to the ground, when Cleocatra reappeared. She apologised that the Sphinx wasn't any more help, but she had found out that the answer could be with the King of cats. The King of cats, Cleocatra continued, was a lion. He lived south from Giza in an extinct volcano called Ngorongoro. Cleocatra didn't know exactly where it was, so having thanked her and the Sphinx for their help, Neko and Ahmed set off for the library as Ahmed didn't have an atlas at home. Having consulted the atlas, it turned out that Cleocatra was right – it was south, a very long way south, in a country called Tanzania. Luckily it looked like Neko could follow the Nile River right to its source, close to Lake Victoria which is very close to Ngorongoro Crater.

After checking the timetable, it appeared that a River Nile ferry was leaving the next day. Ahmed didn't think that it would take Neko the whole way to Lake Victoria – even from the map they could see that the Aswan Dam was in the way. The dam had been built to try and control the annual flooding of the Nile and to provide irrigation for the very fertile plains that ran alongside the banks of this famous river.

Ahmed felt that they needed a smaller boat and he decided he had better consult a friend of his called Sadat who was named after a former president of Egypt. Sadat lived with a trader who often sailed up and down the Nile, bearing goods from Cairo to the small towns and villages along the banks of the river. Sadat's job was to keep the rats away from the cargo. As expected, Sadat was found under an awning on his master's dhow which, as far as Neko could see, was a sailing boat. The boat was very heavily loaded with goods, and according to Sadat, was due to set sail that evening for Khartoum.

They sat in the late afternoon sun eating dates and drinking very strong coffee. Ahmed explained to Sadat that Neko was trying to get to Tanzania. Sadat didn't know where that was, but Ahmed assured him it was far south of Khartoum. "Well, actually, if my master still has goods to sell on reaching Khartoum, we will keep going further south until we have sold all the merchandise that we brought from Cairo. Only then will we turn back." Sadat added that he would love to have company on the southbound trip, so Neko once again became a sailor. Sadat arranged another silk cushion under the awning for his guest and went off to see when his master was planning to leave. Neko thanked Ahmed for his help and promised to let him know how he got on. Just as the sun set over the Nile River, the dhow set sail for Khartoum and the pyramids glowed red in the evening sky, making them look even more impressive.

The river trip south was much smoother than the sea trip with Kenji on the *Tōkyō Maru* and Neko managed to sleep. So, while our adventurer slept, the dhow slowly and silently crept up the Nile towards Khartoum and consequently closer and closer to the source of this great river which was where Neko wanted to go. When Neko woke, it was still dark, but by the light of the moon he could see that they had left Cairo far behind and seemed to be sailing through a very dry area. Sadat brought some milk for his guest and Neko thought it tasted different. Sadat explained that it was camel's milk.

"Camels?" asked Neko. "What are they?"

"Well," explained Sadat, "locally we call them 'the ships of the desert'. This dry area that we are now passing through, and will be for days to come, is called a desert. The camels are called 'ships of the desert' because they are able to travel for days without needing to drink water."

Sadat pointed out one such camel, who was standing under a palm tree close to the river bank. "You see that hump on its back? Well, it stores all its needs for travelling for days in there." Neko watched the strange-looking creature as they slowly passed on their way south.

Just after dawn, Sadat's master stopped at a small town to start trading. As they made their way south, the cargo on the dhow changed – soon they were carrying a lot of raw cotton. Cotton was the product that Sadat's master mainly traded in.

One morning, a few days later, Neko awoke to much noise – they had arrived in Khartoum. Like Cairo, Khartoum was a city on the Nile River but much smaller. "Unfortunately," Sadat informed Neko, "my master will be turning around and heading back north in a day or so." Neko wondered what to do next, but Sadat had already made a plan. Down at the market he had found another dhow which was doing exactly what his master [dhow] was doing, only in the opposite direction. This dhow was leaving for Lake Victoria that very evening. Sadat had met her resident cat Jomo, who, like Sadat, was named after a former president – this time a Kenyan one and, like Sadat, his job was to kill rats who might try to eat the cargo. Jomo was a very big cat, even bigger than Lee Roy, so much so that Neko wondered if they were once related.

Cruising to Kenya …

So, once again Neko said goodbye to a new friend and set off with a newer one. After they were underway and the lights of Khartoum disappeared in the distance, Neko explained to Jomo why he was heading for Tanzania. Much to Neko's relief, Jomo knew all about lions and the Ngorongoro Crater that Neko sought. Things were looking up because Jomo had a brother called Simba who lived with a tour guide who often went down to Tanzania with clients on safari.

When they arrived in Kenya, Jomo would find out from his mother where his brother was and when he was next going down to Tanzania. Neko went to sleep that day feeling much happier and vaguely optimistic about meeting the King of the cats. Jomo confessed that he hadn't met him personally but his brother had, which was almost the same thing, as far as Jomo was concerned.

Lake Victoria, the largest lake in Africa, was stunning. All Neko could see around him was water – it was almost like a small sea. The shores were pink, and once Neko got closer he realised that this was because the shores were teeming with flocks of flamingos. These odd-looking birds waded along the edge of the lake, collecting small creatures in their bills which they used as shovels. Their feathers were different shades of pink which, contrasted with the blue of the lake, made a beautiful sight.

Jomo led him off the dhow into the small village to find his mother and, hopefully, his brother. Jomo's mother lived in a sort of grass hut, which reminded him of the one that Tabatha lived in. Apparently, Simba had left with his master that very morning for Nairobi, the capital of Kenya, to collect some tourists from the airport and take them down to Tanzania on safari. Jomo ran down the street with Neko following closely behind. They found the bus for Nairobi just in time and leapt aboard. Once Neko had regained his breath, he asked Jomo what they were doing. "You will never find Simba on your own so I am coming with you," replied Jomo. "Even if we have to chase him all the way to Tanzania!"

At each village they stopped at, Jomo dashed out to find out how long it had been since his brother had passed through. Luckily, it appeared that Simba's master was in no hurry so they would hopefully catch up with them in Nairobi, if not before. The look on Simba's face when the bus drove past him, with Jomo and Neko waving, was a picture. Simba managed to make out 'See you at the thorn tree!' before the bus, Jomo and Neko had disappeared in a cloud of dust. Once in Nairobi, Jomo and Neko made their way to the thorn tree to await the arrival of Simba. The thorn tree, Jomo explained, was a famous landmark in Nairobi and an ideal meeting place. It was, as its name suggested, a tree covered in thorns – its only defence against various animals. Only a few wild animals with very tough mouths, like elephants, giraffe and kudu, could eat the thorns and the very succulent leaves that the thorns protected.

The reason that this tree was such a famous meeting place was that it was in the middle of a restaurant. Simba arrived about half an hour later, asking many questions, mainly to do with why his brother was in Nairobi with a strange-looking cat with no tail.

Jomo filled Simba in on the story so far, concluding with his meeting up with Neko in Khartoum. Simba explained that his master was leaving the following day for Tanzania, and Neko was welcome to come join them. They were taking some tourists down to Mount Kilimanjaro and the Ngorongoro Crater. Simba went on to say that he had met the King of cats but frankly wasn't very impressed – all they seemed to do was laze about all day. They didn't even catch their own food; the lionesses did all the hunting! To Neko, the King of the cats sounded just like his old master, Sato-san.

The trip down the crater was by Land Rover, which Simba warned was not going to be comfortable, and it wasn't. Neko bumped and bounced for three days, until he saw a very large Mount Fuji which turned out to be Mount Kilimanjaro – the largest volcano in the world and the highest point in Africa. Even though it was almost on the equator, it was snow-capped all year round. It rose up amongst the bush and thorn trees like an enormous upside-down cupcake. Neko wondered if Mount Fuji had been copied from Mount Kilimanjaro and his progress was delayed while the tourists took photos of the famous volcano.

Finally, they arrived at Ngorongoro Crater. Neko wasn't sure quite what to expect. Surely the King of cats didn't live in a very large hole in the ground? That is exactly what the Ngorongoro Crater was. At the bottom of the crater, in the middle of a large plain, was a lake. Much smaller than Lake Victoria, it too had the 'pink flamingo fringe'. The descent was steep and therefore slow and Simba explained that although a large number of animals migrated each year to Kenya, following the rains and good grazing, many stayed here all year round, including the King of the cats – the lion.

They found him doing exactly what Simba said he would be doing – lazing under a thorn tree. Very impressive he was, his black-tipped mane forming a cushion for his magnificent head. His tail, which Neko noticed straight away, was thick and powerful and twitched slightly as he raised his head to observe his visitors. Around him four lionesses lay, looking after their cubs, who romped around their mothers. Even THEY had tails, Neko noticed, as they climbed over each other trying to reach their mother's milk. Occasionally, when they annoyed their mother too much, she would swipe them with her enormous paw, sending them sprawling in a cloud of dust. This didn't seem to dissuade them – they bounded up again to feed further.

The King of cats pondered Neko's problem for a while and then, shaking his great head, confessed that he didn't have the answer to Neko's mystery.

His only comment was that south of Kenya was a country called South Africa where the cradle of humankind was situated. If that is where it all started then could this place possibly have the answer to Neko's question? How Neko was going to get to South Africa he did not know. Luckily Simba stepped in and said that some of his master's clients came from South Africa and they arrived by plane into Nairobi.

Before our travellers left the King, he invited them to join him and his pride for a banquet of raw zebra. Neko and Simba both declined as they did not wish to miss their return lift to Nairobi with the tourists. Actually, if the truth be known, neither Neko nor Simba fancied raw zebra for supper.

The return trip to Nairobi was much quicker due to the fact that the tourists all slept. Neko wondered if they might be Japanese because he knew from experiences of his master that he could sleep anywhere. The thought of his master made him sad, and he wondered if they were still in America and safe and missing him.

Simba's master's tourists were leaving that night from Nairobi airport so Neko and Simba would be able to investigate the chance of a flight to Johannesburg, the largest city in South Africa. They found an old freighter which was taking mining equipment to Johannesburg, so the writing on the cases said.

Neko sneaked onboard and settled down between the crates. This flight, thankfully, was short – a few hours – and nothing like the luxury of the flight from New York to Paris. No stewardess; however, on the up side, no large lady either.

The flight was noisy and bumpy as they flew just above the tree tops and over the vast plains of Africa. Neko saw herds of wildebeest and zebra moving across the bush veld seeking fresh grazing after the rains. He saw large rivers, lakes, and a huge waterfall before finally seeing lots of man-made hills and the lights of Johannesburg.

While the crates of mining equipment were unloaded from the plane Neko took his chance to explore around the hanger. Nelson was sitting next to a forklift truck, watching the planes land at this busy airport when Neko saw him. He was an old cat with a very kind face, a very bright shirt and a lovely smile; Neko knew instantly that he had found a new friend. "Welcome to Jozi, the City of Gold" Nelson said with a warm smile. "How can I help you?"

Neko told his story while Nelson sat quietly listening, inclining his head slightly and nodding as the tale unfolded. Neko realised that he had found a wise, patient and kind cat, almost statesman-like. At the end of the story Nelson thought for a while then explained that, yes, Neko was close to the cradle of humankind and they could visit the site tomorrow. However, tonight Neko needed to rest and join him for supper.

Supper was a Braai which is like a BBQ or as they call it in Japan "Yaki Niku", a very traditional South African event. An event it was. Very quickly the word spread that Nelson had an overseas visitor and he was having a Braai. Soon the fires were alight and the aroma of cooking meat wafted through the air.

Neko noticed that the gathering of cats was similar to the one in Greece with Playcat and Arcatmedes, except here in Johannesburg all the cats were different colours like those of the rainbow, and all shapes and sizes. The pots were soon boiling and a stiff maize porridge called 'pap' was cooking.

While everybody tucked into the feast of meat and pap, Nelson explained to the gathering the reason for Neko's visit and his journey up to now. Neko needed help, Nelson explained, and he asked the group if any cat was able to help.

Another elder cat wearing what Neko thought was a tea cosy cleared his throat and pointed at a very well groomed cat in a green and gold rugby shirt. The cat with the colourful hat on was call Bish because he lived with a famous bishop, Neko later found out. Bish said that Tabo, the cat in the rugby shirt, could help.

Tabo, who then put up his paw, said that he would take Neko tomorrow to the cradle of humankind which was close to his mine.

"Thank you, Tabo" said Nelson. As the arrangements for the visit were finalised, Neko realised that Nelson was loved and respected by all these local cats. His gentle voice calmed everybody as they discussed the various issues of the day. Neko settled down once more with new friends and drifted off to sleep to the sound of Nelson's calming voice as he chatted to his friend Bish.

The next morning, bright and early, Tabo and Neko set off to the cradle of humankind. They drove in Tabo's smart shiny black car and soon Neko saw the man-made hills again that he had seen from the air. Tabo explained that they were mine dumps: the place where the discarded crushed rock was deposited after the gold had been extracted. Neko remembered seeing gold in London. Tabatha's Queen had lots. Neko wondered if that gold had come from South Africa.

Tabo explained that South Africa was very rich in minerals and most of them were exported to other counties, mainly China.

As Tabo and Neko entered the area Neko noticed pictures and exhibits that reminded him of Greece and Egypt. Even the collection of old bones, that he found out later were called fossils, had tails! Neko soon realised that the answer to his question was not at the cradle of humankind, and expressed his thoughts to Patrick who was chatting to a strange-looking cat with very long legs and a – yes you guessed it – very long tail.

Tabo introduced Neko to Chelsea and carried on discussing football, which they both seemed to be keen on. Neko learnt that Chelsea was a cheetah, the fastest cat and, in fact, the fastest animal on land. Neko admired his magnificent tail which Chelsea told him helped his balance and cornering at high speed. Chelsea was built for speed.

They chatted for a while until Chelsea had to dash off to meet someone. Neko and Tabo wondered what to do next. Tabo said he was hungry and they should have lunch before going back to Johannesburg. He took Neko to a small shop under a tree where they had some fish. Under the next table was a group of visitors, who, it turned out, came from China. Neko's ears pricked up as they were talking about an old cat that was very wise who lived in China. Now thinking about it, Neko remembered that China was a vast land close to Japan.

It would be very ironic if the answer was, in fact, close to Japan, Neko thought. Neko decided then and there that he would seek out this wise old cat in China. Perhaps he could help.

Tabo remembered that the minerals which left South Africa went to China by ship, and there was a freight train leaving every day to Durban, South Africa's main port. Neko said farewell to Tabo and soon was on his way to Durban by train, and hopefully a ship to China. The port of Durban was busy, lots of trucks and trailers moving cargo between the various ships. Neko was puzzling what to do next when he saw it: a Japanese flag fluttering in the warm Durban breeze.

Eastwards to China ...

It was flying from the stern of a ship called the *Kobe Maru*, the same name of the city that his friend Kenji came from who lived on the *Tokyo Maru*. Sure enough, after watching for a while, Neko saw a cat on board. He climbed up the ropes that hung over the side of the ship. The ship's cat was called Yuki and she was from Kobe, just like Kenji. Neko asked her if she knew of a cat called Kenji. Of course she did – Kenji was her brother and Neko could stay as long as he wanted to. So, the pair of tailless cats went inside to where Yuki kept her secret store of sushi. It was delicious, as usual, and Neko was so happy. They talked about Japan and Neko explained where he had met Kenji. Yuki hadn't seen her brother for over a year, so she was very pleased to hear that he was well.

Yuki wasn't sure if the ship was going to Hong Kong in China or not so she went off to check, leaving Neko to help himself to some more sushi and green tea. It was JUST like being back with the Satos, Neko thought! Yuki returned, very excited – yes, the ship was bound for Hong Kong and Neko could stay until they docked in the Asian port. The trip would take over two weeks, so there was plenty of time to talk. Neko once again settled down on a futon – this time with Yuki – and fell fast asleep, dreaming of Japan.

The time spent on the *Kobe Maru* was very enjoyable. All the ship seemed to carry was a lot of boxes so there were no rats or mice, and consequentially no work for Yuki or Neko. They just sat on the futon, talking and eating, and occasionally in good weather they would go up on deck and chase the seagulls that landed on the ship. Our pair of would-be hunters had almost no chance of catching a seagull. The gulls were much too clever – as soon as the cats got close, they would just spread their wings and the wind did the rest, lifting them quickly above the ship with very little effort. Neko and Yuki had to be satisfied with merely chasing the gulls off the ship.

The ship passed Singapore and then turned north, heading for Hong Kong. They would have arrived within three days were it not for encountering a typhoon. This strong storm, which often gets dangerous, lashed the ship with heavy rain and very powerful winds. The ship swayed and rocked a lot, and had to slow down almost to a stop for a few hours while the storm passed. Neko was almost ill – he just lay on the futon and assumed the colour of his favourite tea: green.

The next day, the typhoon had passed. The weather was perfect so the captain of the ship sailed her full speed towards Hong Kong. As the ship approached Hong Kong harbour, Neko was reminded of New York – tall buildings seemed to climb out of the sea, reaching to the sky. This harbour was one of the busiest in the world and the ship turnaround time was very quick. Since the ship Neko was on was only discharging containers, she would only be in port for a day or two. Neko bade farewell to another new friend and set off for the British Embassy, where he hoped to find Marmaduke's cousin.

Hong Kong is mainly made up of islands just off the coast of China. It was still a long way from Beijing, however, which was where Neko needed to go. Finding Marmaduke's cousin was very easy, because he lived on top of the highest point of Hong Kong Island, which was called Victoria Peak. To get there, Neko took a trip on the Peak Tram, a funicular railway which went straight up the side of the hill. At the top, amongst others, was a very large white house where Neko though a cousin of Marmaduke could live. Neko climbed up the wall and waited to see if he could spot a cat. Suddenly, there was a lot of barking and sniffing and two Labradors arrived. They tried to jump up and grab Neko, but luckily he knew he was safe as the wall was too high for them to reach him. The next minute, both dogs started retreating and up sauntered a ginger cat. He quickly jumped up to where Neko was sitting. "What are you doing here?" he asked. Before Neko could answer, the local cat saw his stump. "You must be Neko! Marmaduke told me all about you and said that you might drop in. My name is Jardine. Would you like some tea?"

Neko expected a similar tea to the type that Marmaduke and Tabatha served. When it arrived, however, it was a kind of mixture of English tea and Japanese green tea. Later, Neko found out that it was actually Chinese tea, made from jasmine, the sweet-smelling flower. Neko explained that he had travelled to Greece, Egypt and Kenya since seeing Marmaduke, but was no closer to finding the answer to his problem. Neko went on, mentioning Catfucius whom the King of the cats had said might be able to help.

"So, you want to go to the mainland?" Jardine asked. "That's what people in Hong Kong call China," he explained. "The quickest way is obviously by plane. I'll check if the Ambassador is scheduled to fly upcountry in the next day or so." As he left, he told Neko to make himself at home and not to worry about the two dogs. "They are called Tai and Pan and apart from making a lot of noise, they are harmless. Anyway, now that they know you are a friend of mine, they won't bother you."

Neko decided to take this opportunity to have a look around. The house was very grand and some of it was very much like the house where Marmaduke lived in London. Other parts of the house were quite different, resembling a house in Japan. This was very reassuring, and made Neko feel closer to home. He settled down on a large rug and sipped some more of this new tea.

Jardine returned with good news. The Ambassador was due to leave the following morning for Beijing, the capital of China. Jardine was sure he would be able to sneak Neko on board and decided that he would accompany Neko on his trip. And so, the next day, Jardine and Neko were heading north. The flight wasn't long, and a little later on Neko and his new guide were heading west of Beijing in search of Catfucius.

The wall that the King of the cats had mentioned was actually the Great Wall of China, an enormous wall built by the Chinese thousands of years ago to keep their enemies out. Jardine had done his homework and said that Catfucius was a very old, wise cat who lived in a part of the wall close to Beijing.

Catfucius was quite easy to find. Like Playcat and Arcatmedes, they found him talking to a group of cats on top of the wall, all of whom were basking in the oriental sunshine. Neko's arrival stopped the discussion while the cats looked at him. Catfucius called him closer. He was very old and his eyesight wasn't as good as it used to be. He sat for a while in silence, thinking and looking at Neko. He then said almost the same thing that the Sphinx had.

"Yes, there is an answer to your question, but I am afraid that it's not here. It's in Japan."

Neko was stunned. "In Japan?" he exclaimed. "You mean I have travelled around the world, through all these countries and the answer has been in Japan all the time?"

"Well you see, Neko," Catfucius explained, "the journey that you are on is a learning process. Each place you have visited you have made new friends and learnt something different. Everything is connected – if you hadn't met Lee Roy, you wouldn't have gone to France and learnt about the corgis and the Sphinx and so on. Now you are in China, listening to an old cat who is telling you that the answer is, in fact, back in your home country."

Neko sat in silence. He was extremely puzzled. He had travelled almost around the world in search of his tail and now he had to return to Japan, his home, to solve the mystery. He thanked Catfucius for his help, and he and Jardine set off back to Beijing.

Homerun to Tokyo…

The return journey to Beijing was quiet. Neko just followed along behind Jardine, lost in thought. Yes, he was glad to be going back to Japan, but now that the answer was so close he was anxious about finding out what had actually happened to his tail.

With all the practice that Neko had recently had, sneaking on board a plane to Tokyo was actually very easy. Once again he bade farewell to a new friend, and just before leaving he asked Jardine to pass on his best regards to Marmaduke and thank him for all his help.

As an experienced traveller, Neko had checked prior to boarding that the aircraft was a Japanese airline. Once the flight took off, Neko settled down to enjoy some sushi. It was great – very fresh, having just been flown in that very morning from Tokyo. The green tea, the first Neko had enjoyed since the *Kobe Maru*, was refreshing – as usual.

A few hours later, Neko had all four paws firmly planted on Japanese soil. He was back, sitting on the tarmac at Narita airport! The trip into Tokyo took almost as long as the flight from China. He had managed to sneak onto one of the limousine buses that ran between the airport and the best hotels in Tokyo. As they got closer, Neko saw the Tokyo Tower again, and it reminded him of Paris and his friends Pierre, Chantel and Maurice. The bus slowly made its way through the city. It passed a travel agency with its bright posters advertising trips to New York, Greece and Egypt. Neko looked at the pictures and wondered what Lee Roy, Dimitri and Sadat were doing at that very moment. It seemed that the bus was taking him down memory lane, because before it arrived at the first hotel it passed a red London bus that had been turned into a bar and shop that sold things from Africa! Neko remembered Tabatha; was she still sitting under the throne in the palace? Was Busby still asleep in the guard house and was Jomo still sailing up and down the Nile River, killing rats for his master?

When, finally, the bus stopped at the Palace Hotel, our traveller got off. Since he was very close to the Imperial Palace, he decided that he would visit an old friend called Mariko. She lived in the Imperial Palace and was basically a Japanese version of Tabatha. She loved all the pomp and ceremony that went with living with the Japanese royal family. Neko found her sitting on a futon, looking out of the window. She was very surprised to see Neko – there was a rumour that he was lost somewhere in America. His family, the Satos, had returned from America a few days ago, she told him. When some of his friends went to see him, they found out that he hadn't returned with the family. The Sato family were apparently very worried about him and extremely upset at losing their beloved cat.

It took a long time to explain to Mariko where he had been, who he had met and what he had found out. Then, when he explained why he had embarked on the trip in the first place, Mariko could not believe that all other cats around the world had tails, even tiny lion cubs. Neko had hoped that, as Catfucius had promised, the answer was in Tokyo. He had gone to the most powerful household in Japan, but even their cat didn't know the answer.

The only good news was that the Satos were back and Neko could finally go home. On his return to their tiny apartment he was welcomed back like a long-lost member of the family and served an enormous bowl of sushi and a very large cup of green tea. Later he settled down on a futon in the living area to recover from all his adventures. As he reflected on his journey, he decided that his only problem was that he still, after all this time and trouble, didn't know the answer to his (and all other cats in Japan) question. What had happened to their tails?

That evening, the Satos had some Americans over for dinner: people they had met during their stay in New York. Neko sat quietly dozing on a cushion, listening to the conversation when he heard the American lady ask the question that he had recently been asking so many others.

"Mrs Sato, what happened to your cat's tail?"

Neko could not believe his ears, especially when Mrs Sato simply explained that as the apartments and houses in Japan were so small, cats tails kept getting caught in the sliding doors and screens. So, to stop this painful experience, all cats had their tails cut off at birth.

"That's funny," said the American lady. "I guess that's where the saying 'not enough room to swing a cat in' comes from!"

Everyone in the room laughed, even Neko. In fact, he laughed so much that he fell off his futon.

After all this time, trouble, travel and adventure, the answer was actually in his own home! How ironic, Neko thought as he left the Satos and their guests to their sushi and green tea. He didn't mind any more that he didn't have a tail. Now that he knew the answer he was one very happy cat, and what do cats do when they are happy? They sleep.

www.ingramcontent.com/pod-product-compliance
Ingram Content Group UK Ltd.
Pitfield, Milton Keynes, MK11 3LW, UK
UKHW020244240426
12048UKWH00026B/1592